Hilary's Super Secret

Three kids, one friendship, and a bunch of crazy adventures!

#1 *Here's Hilary!*

#2 *Josh Taylor, Mr. Average*

#3 *Hilary's Super Secret*

**Coming soon:
#4 *Gordon and the New Girl***

THIRD-GRADE
Friends

Hilary's Super Secret

by Suzanne
Williams

Illustrated by
George Ulrich

A
LITTLE APPLE
PAPERBACK

SCHOLASTIC INC.

New York   Toronto   London   Auckland   Sydney
Mexico City   New Delhi   Hong Kong   Buenos Aires

ISBN 0-439-32990-6

12 11 10 9 8 7 6 5 4 3 2 1   3 4 5 6 7 8/0

Printed in the U.S.A.
First Scholastic printing, January 2003

To Michelle Nagler and Liza Voges, with many thanks.

Contents

1. Food for Thought   1

2. The New Teacher   8

3. Ms. Foster in Love   18

4. Strategy   23

5. A Plan   31

6. Mountains and Maracas   39

7. Hide-and-sneak   46

8. Guitar Goings-on   55

9. The Plan, Part Two   64

10. E-mail Secrets   76

11. Cherry   87

12. The Perfect Class   96

13. It All Comes Out   107

14. The Final Plan   114

Hilary's Super Secret

1
Food for Thought

I glanced up at the clock above the blackboard. *Argh!* Ten minutes to go till lunchtime. I was so hungry, my stomach hurt! I'd worked off the bowl of corn crunchies I'd eaten for breakfast during morning recess, beating everyone at wall-ball. And it didn't help that my teacher, Ms. Foster, had been talking for the past twenty minutes about the five food groups and the digestive system. I would've given up a whole month's allowance to have a serving from just *one* of those food groups right now. Even the fruits and vegetables one.

I doodled a large double-cheese pizza on a corner of my desk, then erased it with my big pink eraser.

"Hilary?" Ms. Foster was staring at me. "Do you think you could answer the question, please?"

"Wh-what question?" I stuttered. I'd been thinking so hard about my empty stomach I hadn't heard her.

A few kids snickered. My friend Josh rolled his eyes at me. He told me once that when my mind wanders, it just keeps going. I hate to admit it, but he's right.

Ms. Foster frowned. "I asked you for the

name of the food canal that carries food to your stomach."

I flipped my pink eraser from one hand to the other. *I should know this one,* I thought. *Something, something uh-GUS,* I remembered. And I was sure the word started with a vowel. "Asparagus?" I said.

Everyone laughed.

Ms. Foster shook her head. "I'm afraid not, Hilary."

Realizing what I'd said, my face grew warm. *Argh!* Why hadn't I kept my big mouth shut? I don't even *like* asparagus unless it is smothered in mayonnaise. *No, wait!* I wanted to yell. *I know that's not it!* But Ms. Foster had already called on Gordon to give the answer.

Gordon flashed me an apologetic look before he answered Ms. Foster's question. "I

believe that canal is called the esophagus,"
he said.

I slapped my forehead. *Of course!*

Gordon's really smart. Sometimes he
talks like a grown-up, though, and he's kind
of a teacher's pet, too. But once you get to
know him, you realize he's A-okay. He and
Josh are my best friends.

When the lunch bell finally rang, I ran to
the back of the room and grabbed my lunch
sack from the shelf above the coatracks.
Gordon and Josh joined me at my desk. We
always eat lunch together. Unwrapping my
tuna fish sandwich, I took a big bite.

"Hungry?" Josh asked, unwrapping his own sandwich.

I swallowed, then nodded.

Josh grinned, and his stick-out ears stuck out even more. They look like two big mushrooms growing out of the sides of his head. He can make them wiggle just by thinking about it. "Know what would taste good to me right now?" he said.

"No, what?"

"A big plate of esophagus, covered in mayonnaise."

Gordon let out a big laugh.

I glared at him, then socked Josh in the shoulder. But I wasn't *really* mad at them because we're always teasing each other about stuff.

Gordon flapped his arms like chicken wings. "What Josh said *was* pretty funny. You'll have to EGGS-cuse me for laughing."

I rolled my eyes at him. Ever since I gave him the nickname "Chicken Boy," Gordon's always making up these dumb chicken jokes.

Josh rubbed his shoulder. "You have an incredible brain, Hilary. It starts working the minute you get out of bed in the morning and never stops till you're called on in class."

I held up my pink eraser. "If I gave you this, would you rub yourself out?"

By now, Gordon was practically rolling on the floor with laughter.

Josh wiggled his ears at me. "Serves you right for beating me at wall-ball this morning."

I snorted. "I *always* beat you at wall-ball."

"*Almost* always," Josh corrected. Then he took a big sip from his carton of juice.

When Gordon finally stopped laughing,

he and Josh started talking about some program they saw on TV last night.

I finished my sandwich and tore open a bag of potato chips. Crunching on a mouthful of chips, I watched Ms. Foster correcting papers at her desk at the front of the room. She was wearing a pair of jeans and an orange sweater. Her dark hair was wild and frizzy, as usual.

Watching her, I sighed. I don't think she likes me as much as she likes Gordon, but I wish she did. Maybe if she thought I was as smart as Gordon, she'd like me better. But why would she ever think that when every time I open my mouth in class, it's just to say something dumb?

2
The New Teacher

After lunch recess, my class walked in line to the music room. Our regular music teacher, Mrs. Marshall, wasn't there. Instead we had a substitute. His name was Mr. Stenson. He was real nice looking, tall and tan, with brown eyes and wavy light brown hair. Slung over his shoulder, a guitar hung from a red-and-black diamond-patterned strap.

"I'm afraid I have some bad news," Mr.

Stenson told us. "Mrs. Marshall won't be back for the rest of the year. Her mother is ill, and she's taking time off to care for her."

Most of the kids groaned, but I didn't. I mean, I felt sorry about Mrs. Marshall's mother, of course, and Mrs. Marshall's okay, but she never seemed to appreciate my singing much. I like to sing, but I've got what my dad calls a "tin ear." That means I have a hard time singing in tune, even though I sound okay to me. I like to sing loud, but Mrs. Marshall makes me stand in the back row, and she cringes whenever I hit a note she doesn't like. Josh told me once that when I sing, people clap their hands — over their ears.

Mr. Stenson smiled at us. "I know you'll miss Mrs. Marshall," he said. "And much as I'd like to, I won't be able to fill her shoes." He laughed. "For one thing, I wouldn't be

9

able to fit into them. My feet are *much* larger than hers."

I glanced at his feet. They *were* pretty big. In fact, if he went water-skiing he might not need to use skis!

"I'm afraid the school district is rather short on music substitutes," Mr. Stenson continued. "I've had a couple of music classes, but I've never actually taught music before." He paused. "I can play the guitar, though." He gave it a thump. "But I'm going to need you to help me out."

Mr. Stenson let us pick a place to stand on the risers, so I chose the front row. Then he asked which songs we'd been practicing, and we sang them for him while he strummed along on his guitar. After each song he applauded us wildly, and he even gave me a compliment for "not being afraid to sing out." Then he asked me to direct one of the songs! It was fun waving my hands around in time to the music, and Mr. Stenson said I did a good job. I never had such a great time in music before.

When Ms. Foster came to pick us up, I didn't want to leave! I wish she could've seen me directing. It might've helped make up for my stupid "asparagus" goof.

"Good afternoon, Ms. Foster," Mr. Stenson said as we lined up at the door. "Do you know that you have a very fine class?"

Ms. Foster's eyes lit up. "Thank you," she said. "I've always thought they were a very fine class, too."

Really? But then she probably wasn't thinking of *me*.

Mr. Stenson winked. "Perhaps they're a very fine class because they have a very fine teacher."

Ms. Foster laughed this tinkly little

laugh I'd never heard before and smoothed back her hair. "Why, Mr. Stenson. What a nice thing to say!"

All the way back to class Ms. Foster hummed a little tune. Then after silent reading and social studies she did something she's never done before; she let us go out for afternoon recess five minutes early.

"I think there's something strange going on with Ms. Foster," I said to Josh and Gordon as we stood in line to play wall-ball.

"Strange? How?" asked Josh.

Gordon raised an eyebrow. "Can you give us an *eggs*-ample?"

"Well, she *never* lets us go to recess early," I said. "Besides that, she hummed all the way back from music."

"What's wrong with that?" Gordon said. "Many people hum."

"But that's not like her," I said. "She's usually not so . . . so *cheerful*."

Gordon rolled his eyes. He probably thought I was trying to make something out of nothing, which is something my mom says I do a lot.

Josh shrugged. "Maybe she's just feeling happy today. It's not against the law, you know."

I gently punched him in the shoulder.

"Hey," he said. "What'd I do *this* time?"

I grinned. "Nothing. I just felt like it. It's not against the law, you know."

Just then, Alicia, who sits ahead of me in class, ran up to us. "Mrs. Crawford sent me to ask you to come to the office," she told me.

My heart began to pound. "Do you know what she wants?" I asked. Mrs. Crawford is the school secretary. The last time I had to go to the office I was in trouble for being tardy. But I hadn't been late to school in a long time.

"She probably found out you were beating up on me," said Josh.

I gave him a look. "Ha-ha."

Alicia shook her head, and her cat earrings jingled. Alicia's crazy about cats. "Sorry. She didn't say."

As soon as I opened the door to the office I saw my mom. My baby sister, Melanie, was asleep on Mom's shoulder. Before I could ask why she was here, Mom handed me a house key. "I forgot to tell you I might be gone when you get home," she said. "I have to take Melanie to the doctor for a checkup." She lifted Melanie higher on her shoulder, then bent to give me a kiss. "I should be back shortly after you get home, if not before."

I'd planned to go outside again after

Mom left, but then I glanced at the clock above Mrs. Crawford's desk. There wouldn't be enough time for a game of wall-ball if I went back outside because recess would end before I could even reach the front of the line. "Can I just stay here till the bell rings?" I asked Mrs. Crawford.

She smiled. "If you don't mind working." She handed me a stack of mail. "How about putting this stuff into the teachers' boxes for me?"

"Sure," I said.

I'd gotten through about a third of the stack when I came across a light pink envelope with the name F. JAMES STENSON written on the front in fancy letters. There wasn't any stamp on the envelope. Maybe it was a note from another teacher, I thought. Then I wondered what the "F" stood for in "F. James." Kids hardly ever get to know their teachers' first names. I didn't know Ms. Foster's first name, either.

I was about to toss the envelope into Mr. Stenson's box when I noticed a sweet smell. I sniffed the envelope. It had *perfume* on it!

I'd almost finished with the stack of mail when I overheard Ms. Foster talking to an-

other teacher. They were standing by the copy machine in the little room next to the office. I couldn't see them very well because they had their backs to me, so I'm sure Ms. Foster didn't even know I was there.

". . . He's such a doll," she was saying. "And he has the prettiest brown eyes."

"Is that right?" said the other teacher. "Sounds to me like you're in love."

"Could be." Ms. Foster laughed that tinkly laugh again. "Could very well be."

3
Ms. Foster in Love

The bell rang, and I hurried down the hall to class. *Ms. Foster in love?* I couldn't believe it! Not that I think it's impossible. It's just that she's my *teacher*. It was weird to think of her crushing on some guy when I was used to thinking of her as someone who just taught reading and math and stuff. As I sat down at my desk, I wondered who the guy could be, and if he liked Ms. Foster as much as she liked him.

When Ms. Foster entered the room, I stared at her really hard. Even with wild, frizzy hair, she was kind of pretty. And her eyes were nice, too. They were the color of milk chocolate — a light, soft brown. And that's when it hit me. *Brown eyes*. Mr. Stenson had brown eyes, too!

My mind raced as I chewed on a pencil. Could Ms. Foster be in love with Mr. Stenson? I remembered how he'd winked at her and called her *a very fine teacher*. Maybe he was in love with her, too!

Then I remembered the light pink envelope addressed to *F. James Stenson*. What if it was a love letter from Ms. Foster? That would certainly explain the *perfume*!

Ms. Foster was smiling at us. "I feel like

doing something fun this afternoon," she said. "Why don't we skip science just for today and play board games instead?"

My mouth dropped open. But everyone else cheered. Was I the only one who thought Ms. Foster was acting strange? She usually only lets us play games during "rainy day" recesses — when the weather's so bad we can't play outside. Maybe this was what being in love did to a person!

I jumped up and grabbed a game from the cupboards at the side of the room. "Come on, Gordon!" I called. "Let's beat Josh in a game of Clue."

"Guess what?" I said to Mom as I was setting the table for dinner that night. "I think my teacher is in love."

Mom took a pan of rolls from the oven and set them on top of the stove. "Really?" she said. "And why do you think that?"

I didn't want her to think I was making something out of nothing, so I told her everything: what I'd overheard in the office, what Mr. Stenson had said to Ms. Foster, his brown eyes, the perfumed pink envelope, and Ms. Foster's strange behavior.

"Hmm," Mom said. "I can certainly see why you might think something's going on." She opened the oven door again and took out a casserole.

"I think it would be great if Ms. Foster and Mr. Stenson got married," I said, wondering if there was something I could do to help it happen.

Mom set the casserole down and looked me in the eye. "That might be very nice," she said. "But that's a decision for the two of them to make and no one else."

Grrr. It was like she had read my mind or something! But what's *wrong* with helping two people who are in love get together? If I could help speed things up even a little, Ms. Foster would probably be so grateful, she'd like me the best of *anyone* in class!

4
Strategy

As I walked up to the front entrance of the school the next morning, Mr. Stenson rode up on a bike. It was expensive-looking, shiny, and black, with lots of gears. "Hi, Mr. Stenson," I said. "I didn't know you rode a bike to school." All the other teachers drove cars.

"Well, hello, Hilary." Mr. Stenson parked his bike in the racks in front of the school. "I ride whenever I can. I like the exercise and fresh air." He unstrapped his helmet and pulled it off. Then he inhaled deeply. "Ahh," he said. "Isn't it a great day?"

I nodded. The sun *was* shining, even if it was a little cloudy and cool. Mr. Stenson sure seemed to be in a good mood. I wondered if it had anything to do with Ms. Foster. In the movies people are always extra cheerful when they're in love.

"Know what?" I said slyly as I walked beside him to the school's front doors. "I bet Ms. Foster thinks it's a great day, too. And I'm sure she loves exercise and fresh air."

Mr. Stenson laughed. "You're probably right," he said. "I'll have to ask her sometime."

"Ask her today," I said, then added quickly, "I just know she'd like talking to you."

We'd reached the front doors. Mr. Stenson gave me a funny look, then smiled. Maybe he suspected I knew about him and Ms. Foster. He held the door open for me.

"Thanks," I said. "See you tomorrow," I added, since it was Tuesday. We only have music on Mondays, Wednesdays, and every other Thursday. I went down the hall to my room.

As I took my seat I noticed that Ms. Foster was wearing a dress today, a turquoise-blue one. It looked pretty on her. And she'd pinned back her wild, frizzy hair with these sparkly silver butterfly clips. For a second, I actually wondered why she was so dressed up. But then I remembered about Mr. Stenson. She must've dressed up for him!

Josh sneaked up beside my desk. "Wait till you see the new serve I've been working on. You and Gordon won't even be able to

25

return the ball!" He rubbed his hands together. "I call it the *Bulldog* serve because it's so *tough*."

I rolled my eyes. "A better name would be the *Wishful Thinking* serve."

"Ha! Just wait till morning recess." The starting bell rang, and Josh scurried back to his seat.

"Hey, Gordon," I said when he passed out our spelling work sheets a few minutes later. "Josh says he's got a new serve, and we won't be able to return it."

Gordon grinned. "I find that *eggs*-tremely unlikely." Then he handed me a work sheet. "My big toe could design better wall-ball moves than Josh."

I laughed. But Gordon IS a better player than Josh — in fact, he's almost as good as me.

At recess time, Gordon and I hurried outside to meet Josh. He was already standing on one of the wall-ball courts, bouncing a yellow rubber ball up and down. "Prepare to meet your doom," he said.

Gordon rolled his eyes. "Do you want to humiliate him, Hilary, or shall I?"

"Be my guest," I said.

Gordon stepped up to play.

Josh spun the ball between his hands, then smacked it hard. The ball bounced, then hit the wall and zigzagged off at a crazy angle. Gordon scrambled to follow the ball, but before he could get to it, it bounced twice.

"Yes!" crowed Josh. "You're out!"

Gordon shrugged. "Mere luck. You'll never be able serve it that way two times in a row."

Josh wiggled his ears. "We'll see about that!"

I stepped up to take Gordon's place. Josh bounced the ball a few times, then spun and

smashed it again. I'd seen what'd happened before, so I waited a fraction of a second longer than I usually would before making my move, trying to guess where the ball would land. Sure enough, it zigzagged off the wall again. I managed to get to it — but just barely.

My return was weak, and Josh was ready for it. He hit the ball hard. It bounced once, then slammed against the wall and landed far back in the court. I couldn't get to it fast enough, and I was out. "Phew!" I said. "That *Bulldog* is some serve."

Josh was grinning from mushroom ear to mushroom ear.

Gordon grabbed his hand and shook it. "I congratulate you on your new serve," he said. "It is an *eggs*-cellent strategy."

When recess ended, we walked back to class. The word *strategy* kept bouncing around in my brain. *Hmm,* I thought. *If strategy could work in a game of wall-ball, maybe it could work in bringing Ms. Foster and Mr. Stenson together, too.* But I had a feeling I'd need help, and convincing Josh and Gordon to give me a hand wasn't likely to be easy.

5
A Plan

Gordon frowned. "I don't know, Hilary. I don't think playing Cupid is such a good idea." He and Josh and I were standing around the drinking fountain in the hall.

Josh nodded. "Playing Cupid's stupid," he said.

"But it'll be fun," I insisted. "And we'll be helping Ms. Foster out."

Gordon bent over the fountain and took

a sip of water. "Maybe she doesn't need our help. Not on this, anyway."

"Of course she does," I said. "She just doesn't *know* it."

Josh rolled his eyes. "What if you're wrong about them liking each other? Mr. Stenson might even be married."

I tapped the ring finger on my left hand. "No wedding band."

"Perhaps he has a girlfriend," Gordon put in.

Argh. I hadn't thought of that! What if the letter inside that perfumed pink envelope *wasn't* from Ms. Foster? But Mr. Stenson sure *seemed* to like her. And even if the letter was from someone else, it didn't mean that person was his girlfriend, right? I glared at Gordon. "I just thought you might like to help, that's all."

I turned to Josh. "Just because you came

32

up with a great serve like the *Bulldog* doesn't mean you have good ideas about other things, I guess." I turned on my heel and pretended to storm off. As I'd hoped, they stopped me.

"Now, wait a minute," said Gordon. "We didn't say we *wouldn't* help. Only that we weren't sure it was a good idea."

I turned around.

Josh wiggled his ears. "I have *lots* of other ideas besides the *Bulldog*."

I grinned. "Then you'll help?"

Gordon and Josh looked at each other and shrugged. "I suppose," Gordon said.

Josh nodded.

Okay. So maybe they didn't seem all that happy about helping. At least they were willing to go along with me for now. "I'll meet you after school for a strategy-planning meeting," I said as we went back to class.

As soon as school was out we met behind the portable classroom at the edge of the playground. We'd gotten in trouble for playing wall-ball there once before, but nobody'd said anything about the portable being off-limits for *conversation*.

We sat down against the back wall, which faced away from the playground, after I'd checked to make sure no other students — or teachers — were around. "I've been trying to think of ways to get Ms. Foster and Mr. Stenson talking to each other more," I began.

"And . . . ?" said Gordon.

"Well, I have this idea. . . ."

"Be nice to it," Josh interrupted. "It must be lonely."

I ignored him. "Each teacher has a box in the office for mail," I said.

Josh picked at his shoelaces. "So?"

"So if you and Gordon talked to Mrs.

34

Crawford to distract her, I could take some of Ms. Foster's mail and put it into Mr. Stenson's box."

Josh raised an eyebrow. "How's that going to get them to talk?"

"Don't you see?" I said, growing excited. "Mr. Stenson would have to go to Ms. Foster to tell her what happened and to give her the mail."

Gordon picked up a small rock that was by his foot. He tossed it from one hand to the other. "Seems more likely Mr. Stenson would just slip the mail that wasn't his into Ms. Foster's box." He paused. "At least that's what *I'd* do."

I frowned. Though I hated to admit it, he was probably right. I drew my knees up to my chin. "Do either of you have a *better* idea?"

Josh shrugged. "How about if instead of

switching mail, we take something from Ms. Foster's room and plant it where Mr. Stenson is sure to find it." He glanced at Gordon. "It could be something so big he couldn't just slip it into Ms. Foster's mailbox."

"Like what?" I asked.

"I don't know," said Josh. "A globe?"

"But how would Mr. Stenson know it came from Ms. Foster's room?" I asked. "There are lots of globes in the school."

"I think they have room numbers on them," said Gordon. "But maybe it would be better to take something from Mr. Stenson's room and plant it in Ms. Foster's room instead."

"Why?" Josh and I asked at the same time.

Gordon threw his rock into some bushes that bordered the playground. "Because if Ms. Foster likes Mr. Stenson as much as you think she does, she'll be the one most likely to return the 'misplaced' object." He paused. "It should, of course, be something he'd be very happy to have back."

Good points, I thought. "But what if she just asks *someone in class* to return whatever it is?"

Gordon grinned. "Who do you think she'll ask?"

A light went on inside my head. "You!" I said. But then I had another thought. "If you say 'no,' won't she just ask someone else?"

Gordon tapped his head. "You can leave that part to the genius of Chicken Boy. After all, I *am* an egghead."

Josh and I groaned. "Okay," I said. "That's a deal." I still had no idea what we would take, or for that matter, how we would get the thing back to our classroom. But it was a start.

6
Mountains and Maracas

When I got to school the next morning, Wednesday, Mr. Stenson was parking his bike in the bike rack. I walked up to him. "Hi," I said. "Did you see Ms. Foster yesterday?"

"I saw her in the staff room at lunchtime." His forehead wrinkled. "Why do you ask? Is there something wrong? I hope she's not sick or something."

"Oh, no," I said quickly. "Nothing like that."

For a second, he looked puzzled. Then he snapped his fingers. "Now I remember! I was supposed to ask her if she likes fresh air and exercise, wasn't I?" He laughed.

"It's okay if you didn't remember," I said as we walked toward the front doors of the school together. "But did you notice how pretty she looked in that turquoise-blue dress she was wearing? And she had silver butterfly clips in her hair."

"Come to think of it, I *did* notice," said Mr. Stenson. He held the door open for me. "After you, milady," he said with a bow.

Grinning, I swept through the door. "Thanks, Mr. Stenson. See you later."

"And he was really worried that Ms. Foster might be sick or hurt," I whispered to

40

Gordon and Josh. The bell hadn't rung yet, and we were huddled together by the coat-racks at the back of the classroom.

Josh rolled his eyes. "Sounds like he's in love, all right."

"So have you thought about how and what you're going to take from the music room?" Gordon asked.

"Not yet," I said. "But while we're in music today I'll figure something out."

Music was after lunch recess. I chose a place in the front row again.

While the rest of the class was still taking their places on the risers, Mr. Stenson leaned toward me over his guitar and whispered, "Ms. Foster says she loves fresh air and exercise. In fact," he said, "she even climbs mountains."

I smiled. Ms. Foster and Mr. Stenson would probably be so grateful to me for bringing them together they'd invite me to their wedding. Maybe they'd even ask me to be the flower girl!

Mr. Stenson strummed a few chords on his guitar. "Thought we'd sing a new song today," he told everyone. "Some of you might even know it." He winked at me. "It's called 'The Bear Went Over the Mountain.'"

Josh was standing right beside me. As I started to sing, in what I hoped was a high, clear voice, he poked me in the shoulder. "Too bad you're not on TV," he said. "Then I could turn you off."

I poked him back. "Why don't you try to act nice," I said. "Or don't you do imitations?"

When we'd finished the song, Mr. Stenson lifted the red-and-black diamond-patterned strap over his head and leaned his guitar against a chair near the risers. Then he passed around a box of maracas, tambourines, and cowbells with drumsticks. I chose a pair of maracas. I thought about hiding them under my T-shirt at the end of music and sneaking them back to the room. But that might look weird. And they'd probably shake when I moved. It'd sound like I had a rattlesnake under my shirt! Besides, I wasn't sure if Mr. Stenson would care that much about the return of one pair of maracas. He had lots of them.

After everyone had taken something from the box, Mr. Stenson played a Latin CD. Keeping time to the music, we shook, banged, or struck our instruments. Halfway through the song, Carl got a little wild with his tambourine. It smashed into Alicia, who lost her balance for a second and stumbled against the chair on which Mr. Stenson had leaned his guitar. The guitar went flying.

Mr. Stenson sprang across the room and caught it before it could hit the floor. I've never seen anyone move so quickly. He was faster than Josh's *Bulldog* serve!

"Phew," he said. "That was a close one." He turned toward Alicia. "Are you okay?"

She nodded. "Sorry," she said as she straightened up. Her cheeks were bright red. She glared at Carl, who shrugged, then looked down at his feet.

"It's my own fault," Mr. Stenson said, strapping his guitar over his shoulder again. "I shouldn't have left it sitting there." He gave it a thump. "This old guitar and I have been through a lot together. I don't know what I'd do without it."

And *bingo*! That's when I knew what Josh and I would take.

7
Hide-and-sneak

During afternoon recess, Josh and I sneaked back into the building from the playground. We peeked through the little window in the music room door. Mr. Stenson wasn't there. Most of the teachers go to the staff room to take a break during recess times. I checked the door. It was unlocked. "Okay," I told Josh. "I'll sneak inside and find the guitar. You stay out here, and signal me if anyone comes by. Then I'll hide until they're gone."

Josh frowned. "But what if Mr. Stenson comes?"

"He won't be back till the bell rings," I said, hoping I was right. The music room had no other entrances. If anyone came into the room, I'd be trapped, with no way to escape.

Once inside, I scanned the room for Mr. Stenson's guitar. It wasn't leaning against the chair Alicia'd stumbled into, and it wasn't standing up against the wall, either. I picked my way around the risers, then circled boxes of recorders and percussion instruments and stacks of sheet music scattered around the room. What a mess! It looked like Mr. Stenson could use some help getting stuff organized and put away. Maybe later on, after they got to know each other better, Ms. Foster could help him.

47

I couldn't find the guitar anywhere. I was beginning to wonder if Mr. Stenson might've taken it with him, when I spied a closet at the far side of the room next to Mr. Stenson's desk. Crossing to the closet, I flung open the door and sighed with relief. A guitar case was leaning up against an inner wall. I opened the case to make sure the guitar was inside, then turned to signal Josh that I'd found it.

Josh waved at me frantically. "Get down!" he mouthed through the window in the door. *Argh! Someone was coming!*

Quickly, I shoved the guitar back in the closet and slammed the door closed. If there'd been room for me to get inside the closet, too, I would've. Instead, I dived under Mr. Stenson's desk.

Seconds later, I heard voices outside the room. "What're you doing here, Josh?

Aren't you supposed to be outside now?" It was Mr. Stenson!

"I was waiting for you," I heard Josh say. "I think I left my jacket here during music."

"Well, then, let's just have a look," said Mr. Stenson. I heard the doorknob turn. What in the world was Josh thinking? If he hadn't made up that lie, Mr. Stenson might've gone away again!

The door creaked open, and footsteps came into the room. I crouched under the desk, barely breathing. My heart was beating so loud I was sure Mr. Stenson would hear it. What would he say if he found me? What would he do? If only I hadn't opened my big mouth and suggested this stupid plan. If Mr. Stenson caught me, I'd never be able to explain what I'd been up to.

"Do you see it?" asked Mr. Stenson.

"Not yet," said Josh. I could hear him moving around the room.

"I came back to get something off my desk," Mr. Stenson said. "You keep looking."

I gasped as footsteps came closer to my hiding place. Then the toes of a big pair of shoes appeared, just inches from where I crouched. I heard thumps over my head as Mr. Stenson shuffled through the stuff on his desk. "Here's that note I was looking for!" Mr. Stenson's voice boomed, he was so close. "Did you find your jacket?" he asked Josh.

"Must've left it somewhere else," Josh mumbled.

"Well, let's go then. I need to make a call from the office before the bell rings."

After I heard the door slam shut, I waited a few more seconds before crawling

out from under the desk. Then I dashed over to the closet, grabbed the guitar case, and sneaked out the door.

Josh was waiting for me. He'd doubled back as soon as he could. I don't know how we managed to sneak that big guitar down the hall together without being seen, but we did. We were almost to the classroom when we heard footsteps again.

"In here, Josh!" I hissed, ducking into the girls' rest room.

"No way," Josh said, tugging on his end of the guitar case. "I'm not going in *there*!"

"Don't be stupid," I whispered as the steps came closer. "We've got to hide!" I pulled on my end of the guitar, and Josh came with it.

Fortunately, no one was in the rest room. We crouched just inside the door, beside the sinks.

Josh wrinkled his nose. "It stinks like girls in here."

"Bet the boys' bathroom smells worse," I said.

"Yeah, but at least it smells like boys."

As soon as the coast was clear, Josh grabbed his end of the guitar and raced out the door like a rocket blasting off. "Hey, not so fast!" I hissed, trying to keep up.

We left the guitar in its case just inside the door to our room, where Ms. Foster would find it right away when she came back from her break. "You better promise you won't tell anyone I went into the girls' bathroom," Josh said as we headed out the back door to the playground.

I rolled my eyes. "Don't worry." I may have a big mouth, but *not* when it comes to keeping secrets. Josh, on the other hand, can't keep a secret to save his life.

Now that my plan was working, it didn't seem so stupid after all. Ms. Foster would probably wonder how the guitar got in our classroom, but that didn't really matter. The mystery would be one more thing she and Mr. Stenson could talk about!

8
Guitar Goings-on

Recess ended before Josh and I had time for even one game of wall-ball. We marched back into the room with the rest of the class. Ms. Foster held up the guitar, still in its case. "I found this when I returned from my break," she said. "Does anyone know to whom it belongs, or why it's here?"

Several kids raised their hands. But for

once, not one of the hands was mine or Josh's or Gordon's.

"Alicia?"

"Mr. Stenson has a guitar."

A few kids snickered, and Alicia blushed. They were probably thinking of how she'd almost knocked his guitar over, even though it wasn't really her fault.

Ms. Foster opened the case and held the guitar up by its strap. "Does this guitar look like Mr. Stenson's?" she asked.

"It's his!" everyone yelled. There was no mistaking that red-and-black diamond-patterned strap.

Ms. Foster shook her head. "I wonder how it got here?"

Everyone started talking at once. Frowning, Ms. Foster held up a hand for quiet. "Never mind," she said. "It doesn't really matter. But I'm sure Mr. Stenson must be missing it." She turned to Gordon. "Would you mind taking it over to him, please?"

"Actually," said Gordon, "I'd rather not. I don't think I want that responsibility."

Ms. Foster looked surprised. "Why not?"

"Mr. Stenson is very attached to his guitar," Gordon said. "I'd feel awful if I dropped it."

I gulped, thinking how close Josh and I had come to dropping it ourselves, pulling it back and forth between us outside the girl's rest room.

Several kids waved their hands in the air. "I'll take it!" they yelled.

Ms. Foster hesitated. "No. Gordon is right," she said. "I'll call the office, and Mrs. Crawford can let Mr. Stenson know his guitar is here. He can come pick it up himself."

Gordon and Josh and I smiled at one

another as Ms. Foster carefully slid the guitar back into its case. Mr. Stenson would be so grateful to Ms. Foster for finding his guitar, he might even ask her on a date that very night!

We were in the middle of science, learning how to identify animal tracks, when Mr. Stenson walked into the room. I looked up from my drawing of coyote tracks as Mr. Stenson hurried over to Ms. Foster's desk, where she sat working at her computer.

The guitar leaned up against the wall behind her. Ms. Foster reached around to pick it up, then handed it to Mr. Stenson. They bent their heads together, whispering. It was hard to hear what they were saying, but every once in a while I caught a few words like "can't believe anyone would take it" and "a mystery how it got here."

Mr. Stenson glanced toward Josh and

said something else to Ms. Foster. She stood up. "Josh, would you please come here a minute?"

I drew in my breath. Did Mr. Stenson suspect Josh had taken his guitar? But Josh had left with Mr. Stenson when he went to make his phone call. Mr. Stenson couldn't know that Josh had doubled back, could he? My heart began to beat fast. What if someone had seen Josh and me sneaking the guitar down the hall?

I couldn't hear what Ms. Foster and Mr. Stenson asked Josh, but when Josh turned around to go back to his seat a few seconds later, he was grinning.

I relaxed. A minute or two later, Mr. Stenson started out of the room with his guitar. At the door he stopped and turned back to smile at Ms. Foster. "See you later, Debbie."

Debbie? Ms. Foster's name was *Debbie?* Mr. Stenson knew Ms. Foster's first name! That *had* to be a good sign, right? I wondered if she knew his first name, too — if he'd told her what the "F" in "F. James" stood for.

At the end of the day Gordon, Josh, and I met behind the portable classroom again. I dropped my backpack to the ground and flopped down beside it. Josh and Gordon did the same. I turned to Josh. "What did Ms. Foster and Mr. Stenson ask you?"

"They asked if I'd seen anyone going in or out of the music room while I was waiting to look for my jacket."

"And you told them 'no,' of course," I said.

Josh grinned. "I told them the truth, Hilary. I told them the only person I'd seen going in or out was *you.*"

My heart almost stopped beating. "You WHAT?"

Josh held his hands up in front of him. "Hey. I was kidding!"

"Why, you . . ." I reached over and slugged him. This time he slugged me back, but not very hard. I would've slugged him again, but Gordon pulled us apart. "We haven't got time for that," he said. "We need to hurry if we're going to put the second half of our plan into effect."

Josh and I stopped fighting. "What second half?" we asked at the same time.

Gordon rolled his eyes. "Getting Ms. Foster to return Mr. Stenson's precious guitar was a good start. But we need to do more to make *sure* they keep talking."

"So what's the second half of our plan?" I asked, wishing I'd been the one to come up with it.

Gordon brushed at a spot of dirt on his pants. "Ms. Foster's going to give Mr. Stenson a ride home from school today."

I shook my head. "Mr. Stenson rides a bike to school. He doesn't need a ride home."

Gordon grinned. "If the second half of our plan works out, he will today."

9
The Plan, Part Two

Josh and I stared at Gordon. "What're we going to do?" Josh asked. "Hide Mr. Stenson's bike?"

"Hardly," said Gordon. "We're merely going to disable it."

"Dis-what?" I thumped him on the back. "Speak English!"

Gordon sighed. "We're going to let the air out of his back tire."

Josh whistled. "No kidding?"

"No kidding," said Gordon. And then he explained the rest of his plan for Part Two.

I couldn't believe it! If anyone had told me Gordon Cunningham would ever come up with a plan like that, I would've told them they were crazy. Part of the reason I nick-named him Chicken Boy was because he was always scared of getting into trouble. "WHEN are we going to do this?" I asked.

"Right now," Gordon said. "Teachers always stay late after school. We'll do it before Mr. Stenson's ready to go home."

So we crept around to the front of the school where the bike racks stood near the flagpole. I showed Gordon which bike was Mr. Stenson's while Josh hung around the front doors on "guard duty." If anyone came toward the doors he'd warn us by talking to the person in a real loud voice.

65

Gordon crouched beside the rear tire of Mr. Stenson's bike. First he unscrewed the cap on the little tube-thing that sticks up from the tire and stuck the cap in his pocket. Then he took a pen out of his backpack and pressed the point of the pen against the little stem that sticks up in the tube.

Air hissed out of the tire. Gordon kept pressing until the tire was completely flat. I was so interested in watching, I didn't hear someone drive up to the front of the school until a door slammed.

I jumped, and Gordon almost fell over. He scrambled to his feet just as Dr. Wentworth, the principal, came toward us from the parking lot.

We were trapped! If Dr. Wentworth saw the flat tire, we were *doomed*.

My heart pounded as she came up to the

bike racks. "What are you two doing here so late?" she asked, running a hand through her silver hair. "Did you miss your bus?"

"N-no," I said. "We walk home." Any moment now, I thought, she was going to glance down and see the flat tire on Mr. Stenson's bike.

But she kept looking at us. "Don't you think you'd better get going? Someone at home will probably be wondering where you are."

"I-I accidentally left my backpack at school," Gordon said, holding it up. "We just came back to get it." He turned to me. "Let's go, Hilary."

We took one step away.

"Just a minute," Dr. Wentworth said. She was bending over to look at something.

My heart leaped into my throat.

Then Dr. Wentworth straightened up. "Does this pen belong to either of you?" she asked, holding up Gordon's pen.

I gulped as Gordon nodded.

Dr. Wentworth handed the pen to him. "It must've dropped out of your backpack," she said. "Better zip it up."

"Okay," Gordon said.

After Dr. Wentworth left, I breathed a sigh of relief. "Phew. That was *so-o* close. I can't believe she didn't notice the tire."

"Me, neither," said Gordon. Quickly, he pulled the little cap out of his pocket and screwed it back on the tube-thing.

Just then Josh came up to us. "Is everything okay?" he asked.

Gordon and I nodded.

"Did Dr. Wentworth see you?" I asked.

Josh shook his head "no." "When I heard

everyone talking, I sneaked away from the front doors and hid around the side of the building."

"Good," I said. Dr. Wentworth had seemed to buy the left-behind backpack story. I didn't want to make her suspicious. She knew Gordon and Josh and I were all friends.

Now it was time to *finish* Part Two of our plan. Leaving Josh and Gordon to do what *they* needed to do, I sneaked through an outside door at the side of the building and down the hall to the music room.

I peered through the little window in the music room door. The light was on inside the room, and I could see Mr. Stenson sitting at his desk, writing.

I knocked.

"Well, hello, Hilary," Mr. Stenson said

when he opened the door. "What are you still doing at school?"

"I had to stay late," I said, hoping he wouldn't ask why.

Mr. Stenson motioned me inside. "To what do I owe the pleasure of this visit?" he asked.

I bit my lip. "I've got bad news," I said.

He gave me a half smile. "Not about Ms. Foster, I hope."

"Oh, no," I said. "She's fine." I paused. "It's about your bike."

Mr. Stenson raised an eyebrow. "My bike?"

I nodded. "I was on my way home, and I passed by the bike rack. I couldn't help noticing — your back tire's real flat."

Mr. Stenson groaned. "Guess I'd better take a look," he said, getting up from his desk.

I followed him down the hallway, hoping Josh and Gordon had had time to put the rest of Part Two into action. Spotting them as we headed outside through the school's front doors, I breathed a sigh of relief. Ms. Foster was with them. All three of them were crouched near some bushes by the bike racks, studying the ground.

"Those are the oddest tracks I've ever seen," I heard Ms. Foster say as we came near. "Could've been made by some kind of bird, I suppose. But I've really no idea."

She must've heard Mr. Stenson's and my footsteps because just then she glanced up. "Oh, hello," she said, straightening.

Mr. Stenson and I nodded. "Hi," we said at the same time.

Gordon flashed me a grin, and Josh wiggled his ears.

Mr. Stenson knelt by the racks and

frowned at his bike's back tire. "Shoot! Guess I'll be walking home tonight."

"Trouble?" Ms. Foster asked.

Mr. Stenson looked up. "I've got a flat."

Ms. Foster shook her head. "That's too bad. Can I help?"

"You don't have a bicycle pump on you, do you?" Mr. Stenson asked.

Ms. Foster smiled. "No," she said. "But I've got a car. I could give you a lift home if you'd like."

Josh and Gordon and I grinned at one another.

But Mr. Stenson frowned. "I don't want you to have to go out of your way."

"I don't mind," said Ms. Foster. "But if you'd rather, I don't live far from school, and there's a bicycle pump in my garage. You could pump up your tire at my house and ride home from there."

Mr. Stenson scratched his head. "Well, if you're sure you don't mind . . ."

"No problem," said Ms. Foster. "Let's load your bike now, and then I'll go get my things and we can go."

"Sounds perfect," said Mr. Stenson. "Thanks."

Josh and Gordon and I stood watching while Mr. Stenson loaded his bike into Ms. Foster's car. After they had gone back inside the school we gave each other high fives.

"Say," I asked, studying the tracks on the ground near the bushes. "How did you make these tracks, anyway?" Each print was made up of three long, thin, evenly spaced scratches.

Gordon and Josh grinned at each other. Then Josh whipped something out from under his sweatshirt. "Tuh-duh!" he yelled, holding up a plastic fork. "It was *I*. The Josh-bird!"

I laughed. "I should've guessed. I always *knew* you were a birdbrain."

10
E-mail Secrets

Mr. Stenson's bike was already in the bike rack when I got to school the next morning. His back tire was full of air again. I was bursting to know what had happened during the ride home in Ms. Foster's car. Or after. Maybe when Mr. Stenson had finished pumping up his tire, he and Ms. Foster had gone out for a romantic dinner at a fancy restaurant with candlelight and violins, just like in the movies.

I pulled open the school's front door and started down the hall to class. Ms. Foster was going to be so amazed when I finally told her how I'd managed to bring her and Mr. Stenson together. She'd probably go on and on about how clever I was and how she should've noticed before. Of course, I wouldn't take all the credit. I'd tell her about Josh and Gordon helping, too.

When I walked into the classroom, Ms. Foster was sitting at her desk, working at her computer. I *had* to find out what had happened. I pulled my math homework out of my binder and took it up to her desk. After I dropped it into the "completed work" bin on the edge of her desk, I stood right next to her. "So, Ms. Foster," I said, trying to sound kind of casual, "did you have a nice time last night?"

Ms. Foster glanced up from whatever she'd been typing. Slowly, her eyes focused on me. "I'm sorry," she said. "Did you say something?"

Argh. She hadn't heard a single word I'd said.

Before I could ask again, Mark and Carl started yelling at the back of the room. Ms. Foster stood up. "Excuse me a minute, Hilary." She rushed off to see what was going on.

I didn't *mean* to read what she'd been typing, but the screen was right in front of me, and the words just sort of jumped out. Once I started reading, I couldn't stop. She'd been writing an e-mail, and it was addressed to someone named Allison.

Hi, Allison, I read. *Last night with Freddie was so much fun.*

So that's what the "F" stood for! *Freddie.* Hmm. I'd imagined Mr. Stenson's first name would be something less "cute." Oh, well.

I glanced around the room. Ms. Foster was trying to calm Mark and Carl down. Several other kids were at the coatracks, hanging up jackets and backpacks. Gordon was sitting at his desk with his nose in a book, but Josh still hadn't arrived.

In a couple more minutes the bell would ring. Hurriedly, I glanced back at the computer screen and read on. *He's so sweet; I am head over heels in love with him!* My eyes almost popped out. This was even better than Josh and Gordon and I could've hoped for! *After dinner we spent the whole evening snuggled together on the couch, watching TV.* My face grew warm. *He has this spot, just behind his left ear. He loves to have me . . .* And that was as much as Ms. Foster had had time to write.

He loves to have her what? I thought as the bell rang, and I dashed back to my desk. *Kiss* it? Yuck! Grown-ups are so mushy when they're in love. And it was pretty clear that Ms. Foster and Mr. Stenson — Debbie and Freddie — were in love. Wait till I told Josh and Gordon!

At morning recess I finally got my chance. Josh bounced a yellow rubber ball up and down as he and Gordon and I walked around the edge of the playground. Josh grinned. "*Freddie?* Mr. Stenson's first name is *Freddie?*"

Gordon looked thoughtful. "Our plan seems to be working all right," he said. "But

I feel kind of strange knowing about Ms. Foster's e-mail. Like, her letters should be private."

Gordon's words hit me like a sock to the stomach. Letters *should* be private, even e-mail letters. "You're right," I said. "So we won't tell anyone else about Ms. Foster and Mr. Stenson being in love. Okay? It'll just be our secret."

Josh and Gordon nodded in agreement, but a bad feeling stirred in the pit of my stomach. Like I said before, keeping secrets isn't something Josh is very good at. And sure enough, by lunchtime it seemed like everyone in the whole class knew about Ms. Foster and Mr. Stenson.

"Isn't it romantic?" I heard Alicia telling Carl. "Maybe they'll invite our class to the wedding."

Carl rolled his eyes.

Alicia went on. "I bet they give each other kisses in secret when we're not around to see."

Carl made gagging noices.

Then I overheard Stephanie, who sits near Josh, talking to Nicola. "I wonder if Ms. Foster plays an instrument or sings," she said.

"Why?" asked Nicola.

Stephanie giggled. "Because then she and Mr. Stenson could make beautiful music together!"

I followed Josh into the hallway when I saw him go out to use the rest room. "You should try breathing through your nose," I told him.

He wrinkled his forehead. "Why?"

"It might help you keep your mouth shut."

Josh gave me a guilty look. "I didn't *mean* to say anything. It just sort of slipped out. I only told one person. I *said* it was a secret."

I shook my head. "You should introduce your mind to your mouth sometime. Now everyone knows!"

Josh hung his head. "Sorry."

"*Psst!*" Gordon poked his head around the classroom door, then slipped out of the room, closing the door behind him. "What's going on?" he asked. "Carl just told me Ms. Foster and Mr. Stenson are engaged! He said Alicia caught them kissing when they thought no one was around to see."

I groaned. "See what you started?" I said to Josh.

He flashed me a dopey smile. "All right, already. I said I was sorry." He glanced from

me to Gordon. "Would it make you feel any better if I said I was a perfect idiot?"

Gordon looked up at the ceiling. "No, and that wouldn't be true," he said. "No one is perfect."

11
Cherry

Last Thursday was a P.E. Thursday, so today we had music. Ms. Foster dropped us off at the door to the music room, but she didn't stick around. That kind of surprised me. After last night, and what she'd written in her e-mail letter about Mr. Stenson — Freddie, that is — I would've thought she'd stay. I didn't think she'd heard any of the whispered rumors about her and Mr. Stenson, though. Otherwise, she would've said something to the class.

About halfway through music a tall, slim woman came into the room. She was wearing a white blouse and a black skirt, and she was carrying a small, thin instrument case. Mr. Stenson didn't see or hear her right away because he had his back to her and we were singing.

The woman was kind of pretty. Her straight blond hair was parted down the middle and held back with shiny red barrettes that matched her shoes. She wore big gold hoops in her ears. As I watched, she sat down in a chair near the door, opened up her case, and started to put a flute together.

When we finished singing, Alicia nodded her head toward the door. "Mr. Stenson. Someone's here."

Mr. Stenson turned so fast, he almost

banged his guitar, which was slung around his neck as usual, on his music stand. "You made it!" he said to the woman with the flute. "I'm so glad!" He clapped his hands together, then turned back to us, beaming.

"We have a special visitor today," Mr. Stenson said. "Cherry Burton is a professional musician, a member of the Northwest Chamber Orchestra."

The woman smiled at us as she rose from her chair. "Hi," she said.

"I've asked Cherry here as a special treat today. We're going to play something for you." Mr. Stenson adjusted the diamond-patterned strap on his shoulder, then strummed a few chords.

Cherry walked over to stand near Mr. Stenson. "This tune is called 'The Irish Washerwoman,'" she said. "It's a very old folk song. I hope you'll enjoy it." She nodded to Mr. Stenson, then brought her flute up to her lips.

Mr. Stenson began to count, tapping his foot. On the count of four he and Cherry launched into the song. It had what Mrs. Marshall would've called a *lively melody*. Cherry's fingers flew over the keys of her flute. Mr. Stenson played along on his guitar. The two of them sounded beautiful together. I wondered how much time they'd had to spend with each other practicing the song, and suddenly I wished Ms. Foster played the flute.

When the song ended, everyone clapped loudly, and a few kids even whistled. Cherry bowed and said, "Thank you very much." Smiling at Mr. Stenson, she took hold of his hand, and they bowed together. Then Mr. Stenson gave Cherry a great big hug.

I drew in my breath. What would Ms. Foster think if she'd seen *that*?

I glared at Cherry as class ended and everyone began filing off the risers. "What kind of a stupid name is *Cherry*," I whispered to Josh and Gordon as we lined up at the door behind Alicia. "Sounds like she's a piece of fruit, not a person."

Josh laughed. "Could be worse. What if her name was *Banana* or *Apple*?"

"Or *Grapefruit*," said Gordon.

Alicia interrupted. "I think Cherry is a nice name."

Before Ms. Foster arrived to pick us up,

Mr. Stenson asked me and Alicia if we could stay behind for a while and help sort sheet music. He said Cherry had offered to stay and help because two of his classes were on a field trip and he had a whole hour before his next class. "We could use a couple of good assistants," he said.

"Ms. Foster's *really* good at sorting," I said slyly. "I bet she'd help you after school sometime."

"Oh, I'm sure she has plenty of her own work to do," said Mr. Stenson. "But if you don't want to stay and help, that's okay. I can ask someone else."

"No, I'll stay," I said quickly. I really did want to help.

When Ms. Foster arrived to pick up the class, Mr. Stenson introduced her to Cherry. Ms. Foster acted real nice to Cherry. But maybe she wouldn't have, if she'd known about the *hug*. Ms. Foster said it was fine if Alicia and I stayed to help out. She even said we could miss all of social studies and stay through afternoon recess if we wanted to.

There was a ton of music to sort. "Why don't we lay it out on the floor in alphabetical order by title?" Cherry suggested. "Titles that start with A through G could be in the top row. And we could have three more rows below."

"Should we ignore 'A,' 'An,' and 'The,' if that's the first word of the title?" asked Alicia. Ms. Gardner, the librarian, had taught us that rule for looking up titles of books on the library computers.

"Good idea," said Cherry.

"How about if we each have our own row, since there are four rows and four of us?" I said.

Cherry smiled at me. "Great thinking."

She touched the sleeve of Mr. Stenson's shirt. "You sure picked the right students to help."

Without wanting to, I was starting to like her.

First, we sorted all the music by row. Then I took all the music for the second row, H–N, and started sorting through it and laying it out.

"There sure are a lot of copies of 'Jingle Bell Rock,' " I said.

"It's a popular tune," said Mr. Stenson.

"Speaking of bells," said Cherry, "I think I've finally found the perfect dress for . . ." All of a sudden her voice trailed off.

I glanced up. Mr. Stenson was looking at Cherry and holding a finger to his lips.

Bells? Dresses? What was she about to say?

Alicia must've been wondering the same thing. "Perfect dress for *what*?" she asked.

"Oops, sorry," Cherry said, looking at Mr. Stenson.

He shrugged. "It's okay, I guess. It would've come out eventually, anyway."

WHAT would've come out? They were driving me crazy!

Mr. Stenson smiled at Alicia and me, and then he dropped a bomb. A *cherry* bomb. "Cherry and I are getting married in two months."

12
The Perfect Class

Alicia and I didn't say a word. We were probably both thinking the same thing. *Poor Ms. Foster!*

Then Mr. Stenson started to sing. "I'm getting married in the morning. Dingdong, the bells are going to chime!"

Cherry rolled her eyes. "Anyway," she said to us, "the wedding dress I found is just perfect. It's beautiful, with lots of white lace and seed pearls."

But I didn't want to hear about her dress. I stopped listening as she went on and on about it. Ms. Foster was going to be heartbroken! What about last night? Didn't that mean anything? How could Mr. Stenson cuddle with Ms. Foster and then say he was going to marry Cherry? It wasn't right!

I glared at him. "I have to go now," I said.

Mr. Stenson looked surprised. "Well, sure, if you need to."

"Are you coming with me, Alicia?" I asked.

She nodded, her eyes on the floor.

"Bye," Cherry called after us. "It was nice to meet you."

Mr. Stenson walked with us to the door.

"Is something wrong, Hilary?" he whispered as Alicia went out the door ahead of me. "You seem kind of upset."

KIND of upset? My feelings boiled over. "If you had to take a test to join the human race, you'd flunk!" I shouted. Then I ran to catch up with Alicia.

We got back to class ten minutes before the recess bell rang. It didn't take long for the news about Mr. Stenson and Cherry to spread. Alicia didn't waste any time letting people know what was *really* going on. I wish I'd had the chance to tell Josh and Gordon before they heard about it from Carl.

Josh lit into me right away when he and Gordon and I were outside on the playground. "Thanks to you, everyone hates me now. They're all saying I lied to them about Ms. Foster and Mr. Stenson."

"Hey," I said, "that was supposed to be

a *secret*, remember? It's not *my* fault your mouth's so big you could whisper in your own ear."

Glaring at me, Josh shoved his face close to mine. "If I gave you a going-away present right now, would you?"

I glared back. "Ha! The only thing you ever give away is *secrets*!"

Gordon stepped between us. "Stop it, you two. You're only making matters worse."

I looked Gordon in the eye. "Speaking of making matters worse," I said, "whose idea was it to get Ms. Foster to give Mr. Stenson a ride home yesterday?"

Gordon blinked. "How was I supposed to know Mr. Stenson was planning to marry Cherry?" He scuffed at the ground with one of his sneakers. "So what happens next?"

I sighed. "Someone needs to tell Ms. Foster about Cherry."

Josh and Gordon both looked at me.

I gulped. "Okay, okay," I said. "I'll do it."

Usually, Ms. Foster has to remind us to take our places *quietly* when we come back from recess, but this afternoon she didn't have to. We all sat down right away, took out our colored pencils, and got to work on the pictures we were drawing in art. I think we all felt so bad for Ms. Foster that none of us wanted to make things worse by doing anything that would upset her. The room was so quiet you could've heard a *flea* sneeze.

"Wow!" Ms. Foster said after a while. "I don't know what happened out there that you all came back so quiet, but I LOVE it!"

I groaned. She wouldn't be so happy when she knew the REAL reason we were being so quiet.

I waited until the end of the school day so I could be alone with Ms. Foster when I told her. That way, if she started to cry or something, none of the other kids would know.

I stayed at my desk while the rest of the class left to ride the buses or walk home. Ms. Foster didn't notice me right away. She had her back to the room, erasing the blackboard. When I cleared my throat, she turned around. "Don't you need to get going, Hilary?" she asked.

I rubbed my hand back and forth across the top of my desk. "There's something I need to tell you, only you're not going to like it."

Ms. Foster cocked her head. "Sounds serious." She walked over to my desk and crouched down beside me. "Is there some kind of problem I can help you with?" Her forehead wrinkled with concern.

I meant to break the bad news about Mr. Stenson gently, but I didn't know how. So when I opened my big mouth, the news just fell out. "Mr. Stenson's getting *married*!" I wailed.

"Oh, dear," said Ms. Foster. She looked away.

My stomach lurched. I'd been about as gentle as a hammer smashing nails.

But when Ms. Foster looked back at me, she smiled. "It's not unusual to have a crush on a teacher," she said. "I don't blame you for liking Mr. Stenson. He's a very likable man."

Argh! She thought *I* was in love with Mr. Stenson, too! It was true that I'd liked him a lot — until today, that is. But the only crush I'd ever had was in kindergarten, when I used to chase this boy at recess. He moved at the end of the year — probably to get away from me.

"You don't understand," I told her. "Mr.

Stenson's in love with *Cherry*! And I'm really sorry to have to tell you this, but Mr. Stenson is going to marry *her*, not *you*!"

Ms. Foster rocked back on her heels. "Did you just say what I thought you said?" she asked.

"I think so," I said, wondering what she *thought* I'd said.

Ms. Foster ran a hand through her wild hair. "But why would Mr. Stenson want to marry *me*?"

I blinked. I couldn't believe she had such low self-esteem. "Lots of reasons," I said. I started to count them on my fingers. "*One*. You're really pretty. Especially when you wear that turquoise-blue dress and put butterfly clips in your hair. *Two*. You're smart. *Three*. You're a good teacher. And *four* . . ."

But before I could say what number four was, she interrupted me. "Why, Hilary," she said. "How sweet of you to say those nice things about me!"

I stared at her. "But aren't you upset?" I asked. "Last night he spent the whole evening with you . . . um . . . watching TV. You said you were head over heels in love with him."

Ms. Foster frowned. "What *are* you talking about?"

My face grew warm. "I saw an e-mail on your computer this morning. You were writing about Mr. Stenson." I paused. "*Freddie*, that is."

It was like a light clicked on inside Ms. Foster's head. She started to laugh. "*Freddie?*" she said. "*Ha-ha*. Oh, my goodness! *Freddie!*"

I grinned. "*I* thought it was a funny name for a grown man, too. Maybe that's why he goes by F. James, instead."

"*Jim*, actually," Ms. Foster said. "He

goes by *Jim*." Then she collapsed in another round of giggles.

I sure was glad she was taking this so well.

When she'd finally gotten hold of herself, Ms. Foster motioned for me to follow her to her desk. She sat down at her computer and turned it on. "Pull up a chair," she told me. So I did.

"I should scold you for reading my e-mail," Ms. Foster said. "But I think perhaps — in this case — it would be best if you read the entire letter, instead."

13
It All Comes Out

Ms. Foster clicked open the letter in her e-mail program. "By the way," she said, "the woman I was writing to is my sister."

I began to read. *Hi, Allison. Last night with Freddie was so much fun. He's so sweet; I am head over heels in love with him! After dinner we spent the whole evening snuggled together on the couch, watching TV. He has this spot, just behind his left ear. He loves to have me scratch it.*

I blinked. *Scratch it?* How weird! *When I do, his left hind leg goes up and down real fast.*

Left hind leg? Something was wrong here. I hurried on. *You were so right about my needing a companion. You've given me the best birthday present ever. Thank you so much for my adorable puppy!*

Puppy? Freddie was a *puppy*? I clapped my hands over my mouth. "Oh, no!" I moaned. "I've made a terrible mistake!"

"It's okay," said Ms. Foster. "There's no real harm done. No one needs to know about this besides the two of us."

"But you don't understand!" I cried. "It's too late! You and Mr. Stenson were part of my *plan*. And Josh and Gordon helped. The whole class knows, and when they find

out that Freddie is actually a puppy, they'll really be mad at us. And besides, I said something *awful* to Mr. Stenson!"

Ms. Foster put her hand on my shoulder. "Whoa, Hilary," she said. "What plan? The class knows what? You said what to Mr. Stenson?" She sighed. "Maybe you'd better start at the beginning and tell me what's been going on."

I took a deep breath and began. I tried not to leave anything out — except about Josh and me "borrowing" Mr. Stenson's guitar, and the part about Gordon letting the air out of the tire on Mr. Stenson's bike. I don't snitch on my friends.

After I'd finished talking, Ms. Foster didn't say a word. She just drummed her fingers on top of her desk. Finally, she said, "I understand how you got the idea I was in love with Mr. Stenson. But I still find myself wondering why it was so *important* to you to try to get the two of us together."

I gulped. "Well, I . . . I thought if I could help you, you'd . . . you'd . . ."

Ms. Foster touched my arm. "Go on, Hilary. I'd what?"

I took a deep breath and let the words rush out of me. "You'd see how smart I am, and then you'd like me as much as you like Gordon." I stared down at my lap. "Only I guess I showed that I'm *not* as smart as Gordon after all. And if it hadn't been for my big mouth, he and Josh wouldn't have gotten dragged into this in the first place."

Ms. Foster reached out to tip up my chin. She smiled gently. "What you did was wrong, Hilary, but I think you already know that. You meant well, but it's just not *right* to go around trying to 'fix' other people's lives. Especially without their knowledge or agreement."

I swallowed a lump in my throat. "I'm sorry."

"I know you are," Ms. Foster said. "And I accept your apology." She paused. "Now listen to me, Hilary. There are all kinds of ways to be smart. Gordon does know a lot of things, but *you* have a lot of imagination, and that's another kind of smart."

"It is? I do?"

Ms. Foster nodded. "And you have *leadership* smarts, too. How else could you have gotten Josh and Gordon to go along with your plan? Besides that, you're kind and courageous. If you weren't, you wouldn't be here now, telling me what happened."

I decided not to tell her that Josh and Gordon had *made* me come.

"Know something, Hilary?" Ms. Foster said. "You don't *need* to be like Gordon. I like you just the way you are."

"Really?"

"Really." Ms. Foster gave me a hug. "And just so you know," she said, "I rather like living alone. Freddie is all the companionship I need for now. But if someday I do decide to get married, I'll be sure to let you know."

I smiled.

Ms. Foster rubbed the back of her neck. "Now we just have to figure out how to square things with Mr. Stenson and the rest of the class. But I'm sure if we put our heads together we can come up with a plan, right?"

"Right," I said.

14
The Final Plan

That night I called Josh and Gordon to fill them in on Ms. Foster's and my plan, especially the parts that included them.

"I've heard brighter ideas from my gold-fish," Josh said after I'd explained what we wanted to do.

Grrr! Sometimes I could just break him in half. But then who would want two of him? "Listen," I said. "If you've got a better idea, then tell me."

I waited a few seconds, but Josh didn't say anything.

"Just as I thought," I said. "Now, are you going to go along with our plan or not?"

"Oh, all right," he said, sounding disgusted.

Gordon's response wasn't much better. "Is that the best you could come up with?" he asked.

"No," I said. "We had lots of better ideas; we just decided to choose the worst."

"Ha-ha," said Gordon. "Is Josh going to do it?"

"Of course," I said. I didn't tell him that Josh hadn't liked our idea any better than *he* had.

Gordon sighed. "All right, I suppose I'll *have* to do it then."

We put our plan into action the very next morning. After the bell rang and everyone quieted down, I stood up. "Hey, Ms. Foster," I said, loud enough for everyone to hear. "Did you know that Mr. Stenson's getting married?"

The room got really quiet, and everyone's eyes fastened on Ms. Foster as she sat at her desk.

"I've heard," she said. "Isn't that great?"

Now Josh said *his* line. "You mean you don't mind?"

"Not at all," Ms. Foster said. "I've got another love in my life."

A few kids began to whisper.

Gordon stood up. "Can we meet him?" he asked.

"Sure," said Ms. Foster. "He's under my desk."

There were a couple of gasps, and a few kids giggled.

Ms. Foster reached under her desk. When she stood up she was holding the most adorable shaggy little black puppy. "This is Freddie," she said.

Everyone left their seats and crowded around to pet him. "Ohhhh," said Alicia,

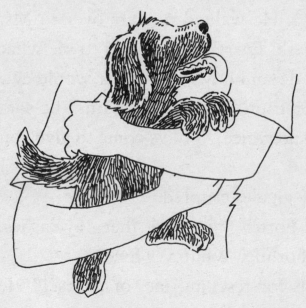

putting her face close to Freddie's. "He has the cutest brown eyes."

"Doesn't he, though?" said Ms. Foster. She winked at me.

After we'd all had a chance to pet Freddie, Ms. Foster put him back in the kennel under her desk. We'd just taken our seats again when the door opened, and Mr. Stenson stepped into the room carrying a large plastic bag. He walked quickly over to Ms. Foster's desk. Everyone watched to see what he would do and how Ms. Foster would act.

Mr. Stenson bowed. "Madam," he said in a dramatic voice, "I have come to give you kisses."

A few giggles erupted.

Ms. Foster fluttered her eyelashes. "Kisses? For me? Whatever for?"

"Why, for rescuing me, of course." He

turned to the class. "The other day I was almost stranded at school because my bike had a flat tire."

I glanced at Gordon. His face was bright red.

"Fortunately," said Mr. Stenson, "your teacher took pity on me. She drove me to her house so I could pump up the tire and ride home."

He turned to Ms. Foster again. "So may I give you a kiss?"

Ms. Foster tossed her head. "Just *one*?" she said. "How about three or four? Or even five?" She paused. "If you're sure *Cherry* won't mind."

"Don't worry," said Mr. Stenson. "I've got plenty of kisses to go around." He turned toward our class again. "Would anyone else like a kiss?" he asked.

"I would!" I shouted.

"So would I!" yelled Josh. He sure didn't look very happy saying it, though.

"Me, too," called Gordon. He didn't look any happier than Josh.

Mr. Stenson smiled. "How about kisses for everyone?" Reaching into the plastic bag he was holding, he brought out a huge handful of chocolate kisses and flung them into the air. Screaming and laughing, everybody scrambled to scoop them up.

Josh and Gordon and I reached into our desks and also took out bags of chocolate kisses. We'd stored them in our desks as soon as we got to school that morning. Tearing open the bags, we threw kisses, too.

"Hey, throw some over here!" kids called out as they caught on to what we were doing.

Our plan had worked great; no one was mad at us anymore!

Later, after Mr. Stenson had left, Ms. Foster asked everybody to pick up the little pieces of silver foil that ended up on the floor while we were eating the kisses. Josh and Gordon and I asked to be excused to talk to Mr. Stenson for a few minutes, and Ms. Foster let us go.

We found him in the music room. "I'm sorry I yelled that stuff about you not being human yesterday," I told him. "I didn't really mean it."

"I accept your apology." Mr. Stenson

shrugged. "Truth is, until I was six I was never sure I was human, either. My big sister always told me an alien spaceship dropped me down our parents' chimney when I was a baby."

I grinned.

Mr. Stenson also took it pretty well when Gordon confessed about letting the air out of his bicycle tire. And he wasn't as upset as I thought he might be about Josh and me sneaking his guitar down to Ms. Foster's room. I bet he would've been if we'd banged it up, though. Good thing he didn't see us tugging it back and forth between us.

Mr. Stenson said that when Ms. Foster called him last night and asked him to help with our plan, she'd explained how we'd gotten the wrong idea about them being in love.

"We want to make things up to you," I said.

Josh and Gordon nodded.

I glanced at the boxes of recorders and percussion instruments and the half-sorted stacks of sheet music still piled up around the room. "We thought maybe we could stay after school a couple of times a week for the rest of the month to sort music, put away instruments, or do whatever else you'd like us to do."

"That's a deal!" Mr. Stenson grinned. "By the way, 'F' doesn't stand for Freddie."

"I kind of figured that out," I said. "What *does* it stand for, if it's okay to ask?"

"Depends," Mr. Stenson looked us over. "Can you three keep a secret?"

Gordon and I pointed to each other. "*We* can."

Josh scowled. "Okay, okay," he said. "I'll cover my ears."

Josh hummed while Mr. Stenson leaned

toward Gordon and me. "It's *Fillmore*," he whispered.

No wonder he goes by "Jim."

On the way back to Ms. Foster's room I thought about everything that had happened in the last week. I'm glad Ms. Foster thinks I have a good imagination, but that's what got me into trouble. From now on, the only strategy I'm going to practice is *wall-ball* strategy.

The recess bell rang as we entered the classroom. "Hey, Josh," I said, grabbing a ball. "It's time for you to get beat."

"Excuse me," said Josh. "Have you forgotten about my *Bulldog* serve?"

Gordon frowned. "*I* haven't."

"Neither have I," I said. "But I've got an idea for a new return. And if it works like I think it will, I'm going to call it *The Dog-catcher.*"

**Three kids, one wacky friendship . . .
What will they think of next?**

**Find out in *Third-Grade Friends #4
Gordon and the New Girl***

The door opened, and Alicia, who sits two seats across from me in class, stepped into the room, followed by another girl. Alicia spoke quietly to Ms. Foster. So quiet I couldn't hear what she was saying even though I sit in the front row.

In a minute Ms. Foster clapped her hands together. "Boys and girls," she said, "Alicia has brought a special guest with her today." She smiled at the girl who stood beside Alicia. The girl had long, shiny black hair and glasses.

"This is María," Ms. Foster said. "She's Alicia's cousin. María is here on vacation

125

from Mexico and will be staying to work with us the rest of the week. I hope you'll make her welcome."

I knew that in Mexico people speak Spanish. I wondered if María knew any English. She hadn't said anything so far, so maybe she didn't. Or maybe she only knew a little. María followed Alicia to the front row and sat down at the empty desk between Alicia and me.

"Hel-lo," I said, speaking slowly so María would understand me. Then I pointed to myself. "My name is Gordon," I said, pronouncing each word carefully. "Gordon," I repeated. I poked a finger at my chest.

María smiled. Butterfly-shaped clips glittered in her shiny black hair. She pointed at me. "Gor-don," she said slowly.

"That's right!" I told her. "Very good."

María laughed. Then peering at me

through her glasses, she leaned toward me. "You don't have to speak to me like I'm a two-year-old," she whispered. "My English isn't *that* bad."

Warmth spread from my neck to my face. *Good grief.* How could I have made such a stupid mistake? "S-sorry," I stuttered. Hiding my face in my spelling book, I pretended to study the words. Why hadn't I kept my mouth shut? If only my mind worked as fast as my mouth.

At morning recess I escaped to the playground with Hilary and Josh. We hurried to be first in line at the wall-ball courts. Josh bounced a yellow rubber ball up and down. "I'm going to beat both of you this morning," he said, grinning. . . .

We played rock, paper, scissors to decide who would serve first, and Hilary won.

"Okay, Josh," Hilary said, bouncing the ball up and down a few times. "Now's your chance to make your dream come true."

Hilary struck the ball with one fist. It bounced on the ground, then hit the brick wall of the school just above the service line and dropped close to the wall. Josh raced to get the return. He hit the ball weakly. It bounced on the ground, then hit high on the wall.

Hilary was waiting. She slammed the ball so hard Josh was forced to run backward to get the next return. Then Hilary hit a soft one and Josh had to run up close again. *Wow*, she really had him running back and forth! Finally, she finished him off with a great shot that landed just inside the court.

"Phew," said Josh. "You sure know how

to turn a perfectly good dream into a nightmare."

Hilary grinned. "There's always the *next* recess."

Seven or eight other kids were in line behind me as I stepped up to play Hilary. Most of them — Carl, Mark, Stephanie, and Nicola — were from my class. I looked around for Alicia and María but didn't see them. Good. I didn't want to embarrass myself in front of María again if Hilary beat me — an outcome that seemed likely after the way she'd just beaten Josh.

I crouched low, keeping an eye on Hilary and the ball. "Ready to be eggs-terminated?" I asked. . . .

Hilary laughed. "I'm going to make you eggs-tinct." Then she tossed the ball in the air and let it bounce on the ground once.

"Double!" she shouted, slamming into the ball with both hands clasped together.

The ball hit the ground again, then bounced off the wall. I'd been watching the direction of Hilary's swing and calculated where the ball would land. But just as I was about to swing, someone cried out, "Come on, Gor-don! Smash it!"

María! Startled, I took my eyes off the ball for an instant and swung too late. The only thing my hands made contact with was *air*.

My face hot, I glanced around for María as I left the court, but she'd disappeared. She had to have seen my air-ball before she left, though. *Good grief.*

"That was a quick eggs-it," Josh teased as I joined him at the back of the line.

I shrugged. As Hilary says, there's always the *next* recess. But I wished María hadn't been watching. She must think I'm a real loser. Especially after the way I talked to her this morning.

When recess ended, Hilary, Josh, and I walked back to class together. "So what do you think of the new girl, Alicia's cousin?" I couldn't help asking.

"She seemed kind of quiet when Ms. Foster introduced her," said Hilary. "But wasn't that her yelling, just before you missed the ball?"

My face grew warm again. "Don't know," I lied. "Could've been."

"Was her name Marcia?" asked Josh. "Or *Mary*?"

"Neither," I said. "It's *María*." Her name sounded musical to me. Like it should be sung instead of spoken. "*María*," I repeated, letting my voice rise and fall.

Josh and Hilary looked at each other

with raised eyebrows. "I think Gordon likes the new girl," said Hilary.

"*Aww, man.* Say it isn't true, Gordon," Josh said. "I couldn't stand it if you started going all mushy on us."

"Don't be ridiculous," I snorted. "I just think she's kind of interesting, that's all."

Hilary grinned. "*I* think it's interesting that *you* think she's interesting."

Josh frowned. "Interesting, how?"

"I-I don't know," I said. "She's from Mexico, of course. That's interesting. And she speaks English perfectly." I paused. "I think she must be very smart. I'd like to observe her and find out more about her."

"*Observe* her?" Josh laughed. "Now I feel better. Sounds like what you'd say if you were looking at a *bug*. Like a rare beetle, maybe."

Hilary eyed me. "Or a *butterfly*?"

I gulped, wondering if she'd caught me staring at the silver clips in María's shiny black hair. I'd never noticed much about other girls before. Could Hilary be right about my liking María . . . ?

About the Author

Like Hilary, Suzanne Williams suffers from "foot-in-mouth" disease from time to time, saying things she later regrets. Also like Hilary, she's sometimes guilty of making "something out of nothing." Fortunately, her family and friends are very forgiving. And though she's not as good at keeping secrets as Hilary, at least she's better at it than Josh.

The author of several children's books, including the Children's Choice Award–winning picture book *Library Lil*, Suzanne lives in Renton, Washington, with her husband, Mark, her daughter, Emily, and her son, Ward. You can visit Suzanne on the web at www.suzanne-williams.com.